DOTING DADDY

A DDlg Instalove Spanking Erotic Romance

Sonia Lake

CONTENTS

CHAPTER ONE

Elyse

Phew, okay. I steady myself as I climb out of my car awkwardly onto my high heels. The tiny spikes wobble as I catch my balance, smoothing my skirt as I look myself over in the car window.

The crushed velvet dress nips in at the waist and swishes around my wide hips. It's a dark eggplant, nearly black. I've drawn my long, wavy chestnut hair over one shoulder to show off the dangling emerald earrings that set off the green undertones in my eyes.

Pretty good. I give my reflection a curt nod and head toward the restaurant entrance.

From what I could gather online, Bistro 57 is a spiffy place. Lots of dark wood and low, warm lighting. I've never been to a place this swanky and I'm fully prepared to make a fool of myself.

I'm not sure why I'm so nervous—it's not like Wayne is a stranger. We've been chatting long distance for three months now.

Don't worry, he's the real deal.

We video chat most days and text all the time. Well, I text all the time, and he gets back to me when he's not seeing clients. He's a private security consultant in Chicago and finally got some time off to come visit me.

We've talked about our limits, our yucks and yums, in explicit detail. And for the past month, I've been following three rules: No beating myself up. No dishonesty or omission with Daddy. And no orgasms without permission.

That last one has been thrilling. It opened up some sexual play via text, then eventually over video. I can't believe someone so far away can have such a powerful effect on me, but my body burns for him.

Wayne is a vision of masculinity — his tall, broad frame is strapped with muscle. His dark beard is cropped short around his angular jaw. His eyes are a deep, cool brown that draw me in like quicksand. And that bright, easy smile, don't even get me started...

I shiver at the thought of running my hands over his warm, smooth skin. Feeling the ridges of the sculpted muscle beneath. Smelling his cologne and his skin as I drink him in.

It's foolish to give in too quickly. I know that. It's easy to keep up a front from a distance.

But it's hard for me to resist when everything I've longed for seems just beyond my fingertips.

Wayne has helped me unlock parts of my submissive, little side that I've wanted to explore. I'm embarrassingly into him and it's hard to reel myself in. Part of me is brimming with hope, while the skeptical part of me is trying to keep the lid on my feelings.

It's either going to be an amazing weekend or a huge disappointment.

Wow, so fancy. The foyer of the restaurant has a high cavernous ceiling that swallows me up. Low, mellow music floats through the background, muffled by tinkling silverware and hushed conversation.

I share Wayne's name with the host and he leads me through the restaurant.

"Right this way, mademoiselle." *Ooh, la la.* I take great care with each step so I don't trip in my heels.

When I see him in the distance, my heart skips a beat.

He's really here, in the flesh. Finally.

He rises from his seat and I see him to scale. His imposing, large figure looks more like a professional wrestler than a business owner. But his luxurious suit is perfectly tailored and gives him an expensive, refined look.

Gulp. He's even more handsome in person. Heat flashes under my skin at the vivid memory of him stroking himself, calling my name as he comes.

"Elyse!" he says cheerfully as he brings the back of my hand to his lips. The whiskers of his black beard tickle the soft skin. His full, soft lips press down gently but the touch echoes through my body.

Jeeze, I feel nervous as a schoolgirl. He helps me into my chair and sits across from me, smiling warmly.

He's cool as a cucumber, the stinker. Suppose his Special Forces training taught him to handle a lot more than dinner dates.

I, on the other hand, am afraid I'll need an extra cloth napkin just to sop up my anxiety sweats.

Cute, I know.

My eyes dart around the luxe, modern dining room and I feel awfully out of place.

There's gotta be some mistake. I'm not a fancy, demure debutante. More like a clumsy little girl. There's no way he wants someone like me.

Old, tired self-doubt bites at me but I know, beneath that, that Wayne and I have something special. I've felt it even from hundreds of miles away.

Jitters slither under my skin and I draw my bottom lip into my mouth. It's hard to believe he's really sitting across from me, as imposing as a solid brick wall.

My body pulses in time with my racing heart. Every part of me is firing on all cylinders and I'm afraid if he speaks to me, I may burst into mist.

Wayne lays his hand on top of mine gently.

"Breathe, sweetheart," he says warmly, running his thumb over the back of my wrist.

Huh, I never knew that area was wired directly to my clit. Funny how each gentle touch sends a demanding pang between my legs.

He's looking me over with those warm, searching eyes. Dark as dusk and twice as mysterious.

"It's just you and me."

His husky voice pours over me, soaking in through every pore. The last thing I want to do is spend dinner skirting around the edge of a panic attack. I draw a breath deep down into my belly and focus on the weight of my body in the chair.

As I settle, a waiter appears behind me to take our order and his sudden presence makes me nearly jump out of my skin.

Wayne gives me a smile that warms my skin like sunshine. I push my nerves to the side and focus on the stunning man across from me.

"Let's start with an order of olive tapenade and steak tartare, please. And we may need a moment to look over the menu," he says to the waiter, who glances at me and gives him a knowing nod. Wayne thanks him as he dashes back toward the kitchen.

"Now, then," he says, taking my hands in his, "sweet Elyse. Let's fuckin' enjoy this fancy place, huh?"

CHAPTER TWO

Wayne

There's my girl. That brought a smile to her face.

She's an absolute vision in person. Just divine. All soft curves and flushed cheeks. It's clear she took time to put her ensemble together and she's done an excellent job.

This place may have been a mistake. I thought it might be too stuffy, but I wanted to take her somewhere nice. Somewhere she hadn't been before.

Maybe somewhere casual would have been better. Still, part of me balloons with pride to know that the most dazzling woman in the room is here for me.

Beautiful as she is, all I can see across the table from me is a jittery, jumpy baby girl. How can I put her at ease?

On our video calls, she's playful and carefree. Even a chatterbox at times. Her doodles and silly texts get me through the grueling days at the security firm.

"It's so fancy here," she whispers, as if she's letting me in on a secret.

"Indeed, madame," I reply with an overly posh accent. She hides her giggle behind her hands.

Fucking radiant. All our chatting and video calls couldn't have prepared me for the magnetic hold she has on me in person.

I lead into a story about my Boxer, Rufus. He nearly rioted when I dropped him off at my brother's house for the weekend.

She loves Rufus — they've met a few times over the phone. The story brings a tentative smile to her lips and it bolsters my confidence.

We talk about her recent paintings. She's a very talented artist and does stunning, large abstractions. During the day she works as a curator for the university gallery.

She starts to bloom, showing me progress images of her new work. She smiles as she shows me the fields of pale yellows and vibrant reds.

I can't help but smile as she picks up steam. She describes her most recent inspiration, gathering excitement and speed as the words bubble up.

She relaxes and we banter easily. It's not our first meeting, after all. I don't know how many hours we talk each day, but it's at least one, every day for three months.

She's got a quick, wry sense of humor that wins me over every time she makes me laugh. Then she beams with pride at my reaction and I feel like the man who hung the moon. Like I'm larger than life and floating on air.

Yeah, I got it bad for my sweet Elyse.

When our nerves abate, I'm suddenly aware of the depth of our connection. And attraction. It's palpable in the room, like a third entity seated at the table with us.

There's a whole different set of nerves firing now. She fiddles with a long tendril of hair as she speaks, guiding my eye over the graceful line of her neck. Her small, delicate hands.

The creeping blush on her cheeks makes my cock twitch. It's good to know I'm having an effect on her, too. It only turns me on more and I scramble to focus on anything other than that damn throbbing between my legs.

If I had my way, I'd send our glasses crashing to the floor and bend her over the table. Take her right here in the dining room, so hard and rough that she screams. Let everyone know she's all mine.

Fucking focus, man.

Back on Earth, the waiter slides our dishes in front of us and refreshes our drinks. I notice she only eats about half her food before she traces lines in the sauce with the tines of her fork.

Poor sweetheart. Probably doesn't have much of an appetite if her tummy's full of butterflies.

I worried about the same, but that porterhouse was done for after I had the first bite. It was excellent.

I've been waiting for the right moment to bring up play time. Sure, we've gone through all the kinky talk from afar, but I want to hear her say the words. To *feel* her getting flustered as she shares her dirtiest thoughts.

That's likely my own wicked desire.

I debate posing the question but I notice she's shifting in her seat.

"How are you doing?" I ask, trying to keep my tone as even as possible.

"Fine," she says with a grimace.

My Daddy senses have determined that that is a lie.

She crinkles her brow like she's in pain. I take her hand in mine and gaze into her eyes.

"Hey," I murmur softly, "You okay? What's wrong?" Worry starts to coil in my chest.

"Nothing. You're perfect. I'm sorry," she stammers, rising from the table.

"I'll be right back." With that, she scampers off toward the back hall toward the restrooms.

Well, the good news is she left her coat hanging on the back of her chair. So at least she's not bailing.

The fact offers me little relief. I can't help but wonder if I did something wrong.

That's selfish of me — I have no idea what's going on. There was pain in her expression, though. Sudden, like physical pain.

Maybe that's it. Moments before, she was laughing and teasing me about my unrefined manners.

"You're real fancy, huh?" she'd leaned in and whispered after I dripped steak juice on my lapel. Her laughter was bright and easy.

Concern starts to knot in the pit of my stomach. It takes all my willpower not to rush into the bathroom and get to the bottom of what's wrong.

If she's not back in ten, I'll go to her, I decide. That's reasonable, right?

Compared to my protective impulse…that fiery urge to storm through anything between us and carry her to safety? Yeah, that'll have to do.

CHAPTER THREE

Elyse

No. Not now. Please, not now.

I knew I tasted garlic in that damn sauce. God fucking damn it.

There are trigger foods in nearly everything, the sneaky fuckers. As someone who can't eat garlic or onions without serious digestive consequences, I don't go out much.

Wayne doesn't know about my IBS. Believe it or not, sharing my very unsexy chronic illness isn't my favorite opener. There's never a good time to bring it up.

On top of that, there's the fear that it'll change how he sees me. Instead of possibilities, he'll see limitations. Brokenness instead of wholeness. A big, needy pile of inconveniences and gas.

This is the last thing I want him to see. Me, doubled over in pain, sobbing on the toilet.

I fucking hate this.

It was stupid to think I could have more. That, maybe for one night, I could forget about my illness and enjoy myself with Wayne.

Of course I embarrass myself and ruin everything. That's all I ever do.

No beating yourself up, sweetheart. His words soothe me for a moment.

A searing, sharp pain shoots through me as cramps spasm all through my guts. God, please let me die here.

The pain and pressure make it difficult to breathe in fully, and the sobbing on top is only making it worse. Negative, self loathing thoughts flood my mind as I weep into my clenched fists.

It's like I'm trapped in a girdle of pain. Cramps pop up from my throat to my rear and all the length between. The gas has my waist bloated out to twice it's normal size and makes the cramps that much more painful.

Tears roll down my cheeks. I need to be home. I need my stuffies and my meds and my tummy tea and my rice buddy.

Anything to soothe this brutal pain.

Damn stupid stomach always ruins everything. Now Wayne's gonna be grossed out and ghost me.

Fuck. Everything. Hoarse sobs break from my throat as I crumple into myself.

"Elyse?" The deep voice startles me.

It's Wayne. Shit, how long have I been in here?

And more importantly, what the fuck is he doing?!

I sniffle, giving myself away. "Yes," I reply reluctantly.

"Tell me what's going on," he says firmly.

"I can't," I wail, burying my face in my hands.

"Sweetheart, please," he replies. The concern in his voice pries me open.

"It's my tummy," I sniffle pathetically. I hear him grunt in acknowledgment.

"Do you need to go to the hospital?"

Okay, pal. "What am I, a Rockefeller?" I reply.

"Elyse…" he warns in a low tone.

I sigh. Time to fess up, I guess. "No…it, uh, it happens all the time."

He exhales heavily. "C'mon, sweetheart. Let me take you home."

It's not a suggestion. Still, I feel like a huge disappointment. He's probably ready to dump me on my stoop and forget this night ever happened.

"I can call a car," I offer. He scoffs at that.

"Absolutely not." Through the small crack in the door, I can see he crossed his arms.

God, I'm furious that this is happening. That this is my body, my life. "I'm sorry," I mutter, wiping the tears from my cheeks.

"It's all right, honey. Let's get you washed and go home, okay? Get you comfortable." This time his voice is low and gentle. Coaxing.

His Daddy voice.

I hang my head as I exit the stall and he leads me to the sinks. After turning the taps on, he stands behind me and gets my hands soapy. They seem so tiny in his.

After we dry off, he helps me slide into my jacket. The impact of each step reverberates painfully through my core. Another strong cramp makes me wince and I cling to Wayne's arm.

"Almost there, sweet girl." A sporty, small SUV beeps unlocked and he helps me into the passenger side. He reaches across me to buckle my seatbelt and tilt the seat back.

The adjusted angle helps with my pain. I sigh as I recline and he rests his hand on my knee.

"Just breathe for me. That's my good girl, nice and slow," he cues as he follows the directions back to my apartment. I'm grateful to obey.

Maybe this will be the day I finally pop. That'd be a fitting ending.

"Keys, sweetheart," Wayne says, extending his open palm to me. I fish them out of my bag and hand them over. With a wince, I prop myself up on my elbows and reach to adjust my seat.

"Wait," he barks as he bounds around the car. Suddenly two strong arms slip beneath me and pull me out of the seat.

He strides up my sidewalk like I'm light as a feather. Once we cross over the threshold into my apartment he flips the lights on. I wince again, but this time from embarrassment.

The place is a mess. I'm used to it, but now I'm looking at everything through his eyes. It looks like an art studio and a play-room made a baby, and then the baby exploded. Yikes.

Wayne carries me back to bed and slips my shoes off. When he spreads a blanket over me, I clutch it tightly and cover my face, hoping I'll magically disappear beneath it.

CHAPTER FOUR

Wayne

Elyse groans and tries to hide after I lay her down. I pour a glass of cold water from the fridge and set it beside her, then head back to the living room to look for Puffy, her stuffed dragon.

The place looks like a disaster area. Sketches, pastels, pencils, cups of murky water and splotches of dried paint sprawl across every surface. Two large canvases are propped against the living room wall with even more lining the bedroom. Her clothing lies strewn about everywhere.

It's perfectly Elyse. Small and chaotic. Colorful. Beautiful. Bountiful.

A couple of possible rules cross my mind that could address her disarray. Part of it comes with being an artist, I'm sure. She'll never be prim or tidy. But she could definitiely stand to be more organized.

Puffy is laying with her tail up in the air, her face twisted in Elyse's woven teal blanket. Poor dragon. I free her and double back to the bed, tucking her between Elyse and the blanket.

"How can I help?" I ask after I nestle the plush toy into place. I wait for her to emerge from under the blankets. When she doesn't, I tug it down gently until I can see her eyes.

She hesitates. "You've already done so much," she mutters through the blanket, looking up at me with worry. I stoop down next to her and bend down close.

She shivers when I lay my hand on her shoulder. "Elyse, please. Let me."

The words come out more sternly than I intended but I see her reaction. In that moment, she recognizes my meaning. It's clear from the emotion in her eyes.

Just like she needs to be little, I need to be a Daddy. To fuss over her and guide her and punish her. By letting me care for her, she's giving me what I need.

Right now, I need to make her comfortable.

"Okay," she says with a note of defeat in her voice.

"There's ginger tea in the cabinet. Could you make me a cup please? And I need one of the blue pills from the bathroom cabinet. And, um, maybe my rice buddy? It's on top of the fridge."

"On it." I kiss her on the forehead and nod before rising to my feet.

Tea. Heat pack. Meds. I put the kettle on and find the heat pack. It's an old band t-shirt, crudely sewn into a small square and filled with rice. There are two mismatched beads for eyes and a clumsy, lopsided felt smile.

"Microwave 5 minutes," the handwritten patch reads. I set it accordingly and head into the bathroom.

The bottle is sitting on its side on the counter. I scoop it up and shake it gently as I approach.

"These the right ones?"

She moves to sit up onto her elbows with a grimace. "Yes, thank you," she strains.

"Lay down, Elyse," I urge gently. "I'm taking care of you tonight."

I rattle one of the small blue pills into my palm and pick up the water in the other. She pops the pill in her mouth so I use my free hand to cradle her head while I bring the glass to her lips.

"I'm sorry, Daddy," she whispers with a fleeting glance up toward me. The word sends a jolt down my spine and twists in my heart.

"Shh, sweetheart. It's okay," I coo, settling down on the edge of the bed beside her. I brush the stray hairs from her forehead and she nuzzles into my touch.

"I'm only upset that you didn't tell me about your illness. If I'd known, I'd have made arrangements. Maybe cooked for us." My voice trails off when I see the tears welling in her eyes.

She bats them away with the back of her hand. "I'm sorry…t-this is not how I wanted this to go," she sniffles before letting out a pitiful cry that punches me in the gut.

I spot a box of tissues on the bedside table and pass one to her, then take her hand in mine. "I know, sweetheart," I say as I scoot close to her. "It's okay. I'm happy to finally be here with you," I admit.

Elyse looks me over with raw emotion in her eyes. Surprise gives way to pure adoration. Earning that kind of appreciation from her makes me balloon with pride.

I trace my finger over the curve of her cheek and down her neck. "You know, just like you feel good when you're little, I feel good when I'm a Daddy," I tell her softly. I run my palm over her shoulder and feel her release into my touch.

"Thanks for letting me tend to you, Elyse. It means a lot to me."

She grabs clumsily at my forearms and tugs me forward, pleading with her eyes. I can't help but chuckle as I lean down and wrap my arms around her carefully.

"Thank you, Daddy," she whispers in my ear. Her flushed cheek is hot against my neck and makes my hair stand on end.

It takes all my might to pull away from her sweet, warm embrace. I cup her face in my hands and kiss her forehead, then meet her gaze. Our faces are so close that I can feel her shallow puffs of breath fluttering over my skin.

"Get some rest, sweet girl. I'll see you in the morning." I tuck the blanket up under her chin and head toward the door. As I exit, I leave it open a crack.

"Holler if you need anything," I add as I back out.

"Goodnight, Daddy," she calls. I wish her goodnight and head into the bathroom.

The splashes of cold water against my face don't quell the flames roaring through me. It's more than I expected, to jump into Daddy mode and take care of her like this. It's having an effect on me.

I grumble as I change from my jeans into my pajama pants, trying every trick in the book to calm my raging erection. Everything short of jerking off, that is.

Last thing I need is Elyse stumbling into the bathroom while I'm having a tug. Don't think I'd recover from that kind of humiliation.

After another round of cold water I settle in on the couch. It's too short and beaten to hell, but it smells like her. Vanilla and lavender, maybe. I curl up and spread the blanket over me.

It's an image of a unicorn in front of a waterfall, monochromatic in varying shades of teal. Fucking unreal. I smile as the fringed edge tickles at my chin. Her sweet, subtle scent carries me off to sleep.

CHAPTER FIVE

Sheesh, what a mess. When I wake, memories of the day before flood over me. My stomach grumbles angrily, but the pain has largely subsided.

Last night opened with the part of me I least wanted him to know about. And instead of rejecting me, he fucking shined.

I've never felt as precious as I did when Wayne doted on me. He's so kind and attentive.

He's seen the worst of me and he's still here this morning. As I shuffle into the bathroom, I hear him clattering in the kitchen.

"Morning!" he calls from the kitchen. How the hell did he even hear me? Damn his Daddy senses.

"Good morning," I reply as I swing the bathroom door closed behind me. I stare into my reflection groggily as I brush my teeth.

That snafu yesterday bonded us more deeply than a perfect dinner date ever could have. My heart is bursting at his generous caregiving. And the memory alone sends a rush of energy and heat between my legs.

Wayne has the dining table set with oatmeal, scrambled eggs, and fresh fruit. Nice and mild for my stubborn, ornery tummy.

"This is perfect," I gush with a mouth full. Wayne beams at that and tells me he did a little reading about medical diets this morning.

Ugh, my heart. I must look shocked because he smiles and turns away, almost bashfully.

"We're taking it easy this morning," he tells me as I pass him my empty dishes. "I was thinking cartoons. At least two hours. Daddy's orders," he says as he scrubs the dishes.

"Sounds good," I chirp back. I practically float over to the couch and turn on my favorite program.

He sings along with the theme song from the kitchen and comes into the room with a big grin.

We laugh and riff on the show and eventually inch closer together. He opens his arm around my shoulders and I melt into his side. I must have fallen asleep there because his voice makes my eyes spring open.

"How are you feeling, sweetheart?" I pull my head up and feel a small damp spot where I'd been laying.

Okay, cool. I fucking drooled on him. Kill me.

"You were out for a couple hours," he tells me warmly. I crinkle my brow and look up at him, unsure if he's joking or not. Did he really sit here for hours and let me sleep on him?

"Guess you needed it," he says, mostly to himself. Then he looks at me and that gorgeous smile spreads across his face.

"Gotta get a couple things for dinner. You feel good enough to come to the store with me?" There's a note of excitement in his voice that makes my heart flutter.

"Mhmm, I think so," I nod. "Lemme change quick," I add, looking down at my pineapple pajama set. They're cute, but now that I'm feeling better, I want to show off a bit.

I throw on a pale yellow sun dress with white polka dots and matching white sneakers. It's perfectly cut to flatter my curvy figure, so I don't wear it much. I don't like that kind of attention from gross, random men.

But when I step out and Wayne scans my body hungrily, I blossom with pride. He has to clear his throat before he speaks.

"Wow, you look fucking gorgeous. Like the...sexy queen of daffodils," he says, then runs his palm over his forehead with a sigh.

Little me, getting big, handsome Wayne all worked up? Yeah, that's a powerful feeling.

He holds my hand the whole time while we shop. We're making honey mustard baked chicken with oven fries and sauteed greens. I'd turned my nose up at the greens, but he insisted.

"No veggies means no dessert." I clammed up quickly after that.

Bossy Daddy. I'm head over heels for him.

We work through the recipe together, cooking side by side. Every brush against him sets off a lightning storm in my body.

The food is fantastic. I must tell him so at least ten times. He drinks up the praise but quickly hands it back to me.

"Gotta give some credit to the sous chef," he says with a wink.

When I offered to help him clear the dishes, he told me to stay put. A few minutes later, he returned with two mugs of hot tea.

God, what a fucking man. My entire body is vibrating with anticipation, longing for his touch.

"How's the food sitting? You feeling okay?" he asks casually.

"Yep! All better, Daddy," I say with a big smile.

A sly grin curls at the corner of his lips.

"Good. Now it's time to talk about your punishment."

Gulp. Of course we've talked about rules and punishments from a distance. But hearing him say the words across from the narrow table has a completely different impact. My heartbeat starts to race as a surge of lust gathers between my legs.

"Okay," I reply. My voice is an embarrassing squeak and Wayne lets out a deep chuckle at that.

"Here's how I see it, sweetheart. You hid your illness from me. That's against our honesty rule."

He pauses and watches my reaction. From the mischief dancing in his eyes, I'd say he's enjoying every bit of my nervy excitement.

"Agreed punishment is lines, yeah?" He runs his thumb over his bearded jaw. His devilish eyes are trained on me, awaiting my response.

"Yes, Daddy. U-usually," I stammer the last word. So smooth.

I hope that now that he's here, he'll give me a spanking. Lines are fine, but I've dreamed of his rough palm delivering blow after blow to my soft behind.

Every cell in my body yearns for it.

"Usually," he chuckles. "But now that I'm here, I wonder if a spanking would be more fitting?"

He can't keep that impish grin from spreading across his full lips. I open my mouth to reply but he poses another question.

"Are you feeling well enough, baby girl?"

"MHMM!" I blurt out, shaking my head too hard. My eagerness is obvious, but I don't care. The wet heat building between my legs is making me bold.

"Yes, Daddy," I correct myself, placing my hands in my lap and sitting up straight. Suddenly I'm on my best behavior. Wayne ticks an eyebrow up at that and shakes his head with a knowing smile.

"Very good." He interlaces his fingers on the tabletop. God, his hands are huge. Another wave of fire roars through me.

"Now head into the bedroom and lean over the bed. Body resting on the mattress, ass up, legs spread. Clear?"

"Yes, Daddy!" I call as I bound back to the bedroom. Don't have to tell me twice!

Oh boy, oh boy, oh boy. I've wanted this for so long. I'm practically bouncing on my toes when Wayne enters the bedroom.

He grunts as he unbuttons his shirt and slips it off. Underneath, I see his wide, muscular chest and the falcon tattoo that fills his upper chest. The detailed ink perfectly accents his stunning musculature.

"Never seen a more beautiful sight," he growls as he runs his hand over the curve of my ass. The heat of his touch piques every nerve and my whole body reaches out for contact.

He teases a thick finger over the wet fabric of my panties. My clit pounds insistently as he toys with me.

"Does my baby girl want to play?" he rumbles.

"Yes, Daddy!" I reply. It's a half whine, half plea.

To my surprise, he assumes a similar position beside me, propping himself up on his elbows and leaning to look me in the eyes.

"You sure?"

Oh, buddy. More sure than I've been about just about anything.

"Absolutely." A smile teases at the corner of his mouth but he shakes it off. When he looks me over, his face is cool and serious.

"Okay. Tell me your safeword."

"Marigold." Don't ask me why. Just the first pretty word I could muster with that would never come up during play time.

"Marigold. And our promise?"

Jeeze, he's really grilling me. A bit of me is impatient, but a much larger part of me is moved by his restraint.

He wants to be totally sure that I'm on board.

"I promise to use it freely, Daddy," I respond. He nods approvingly.

"Good girl."

The first swat makes me jump. They're even and deliberate, but measured. He alternates from cheek to cheek over the thin fabric of my dress, warming the skin below.

My breath hitches when he flips my skirt up and tugs my panties off. The spanks fall on my bare flesh and the sting makes me cry out.

Wayne leans down to look at me, his eyebrows raised in curiosity.

"More, Daddy," I plead, meeting his gaze. I love how delicate he is with me.

I love him. Shit, I love him.

"That's my girl," he says with a smile. A few more blows fall in quick succession.

"Almost there. You're doing great, sweetheart," he purrs.

I let out a moan in response as the pain and heat cut through me. It's as if they're scouring me clean, leaving me pure and new.

"All done. You did so well, sweet girl," he says as he runs his palm over my lower back. He sits beside me on the bed and pulls me up into his lap. He wraps his arms around me and holds me close.

"Daddy wants to know everything. Even the bad things, or things you want to hide. Sometimes those are the most important," he says, running his hand up and down my back slowly.

"I know, Daddy. I'm sorry," I offer, nuzzling into his scruffy neck.

"No need to be sorry, sweetheart. You're forgiven. You're my good girl, always," he coos into my hair.

His word untie knots in my stomach that I've carried for a lifetime. In one way or another, I've always felt inadequate.

Not with Wayne.

He shifts beneath me and I feel the steely bulge in his lap. His excitement goads me on, so I swing around to straddle him and wrap my arms around his neck.

He grunts when I kiss him, but his lips open to mine. I paw hungrily at his back while he holds me to his tight to his chest. The seam between our bodies is red-hot and I moan into our kiss.

Wayne scoops me up and lays me on my back in one smooth motion. Suddenly his huge physique looms over me, his dark eyes shining with desire.

"Please, please, please," I murmur like a mantra as Wayne's hands and mouth ravage my body. His caresses ripple through me.

There are notes of pain amidst the pleasure — a squeeze here, a nibble there. He's devouring me like the most perfect meal, grunting with satisfaction as he draws one nipple between his lips, making me scream.

"My gorgeous, perfect little girl," he growls as he greedily squeezes my breasts. His mouth kisses down the center line of my stomach while his fingers work my hardened nipples.

"Fucking sexy," he growls, kissing the soft mound of my stomach.

Okay, wow. He my remembered my self-consciousness about my tummy. He douses me with praise and I'm utterly drunk on it.

"So sweet, my soft baby girl," he rumbles, sliding his hands down around my hips.

"Daddy's been dying to touch you." Our eyes meet when he says the words and they're fiery with conviction.

"It's so good, Daddy, please," I pant, unsure what I'm asking for. Just *more*.

He nods and parts my thighs with his big, rough hands. Those dark eyes sear through me as his mouth moves down from my lower stomach to my mound.

"So wet for me," he approves huskily. His tongue flicks at the lips of my pussy before diving deep, licking me up and down with long strokes.

A desperate cry escapes my throat and I arch into his mouth. The slick, hot touch of his tongue over my clit makes me throb and tingle all over.

I try to wiggle beneath him but a strong arm crosses my hips and pins me in place.

"Who's in charge here, baby girl?" His voice is strained with lust, his tone firm.

Holy shit. Yum. That simple gesture sinks me deeper into submission.

"You are, Daddy."

"Good girl," he growls.

"Daddy's gonna take his time enjoying you."

Wayne lazes his tongue up and down my folds, teasing me open. His tongue circles my clit with hungry, lapping licks as he slips a thick finger into my pussy.

Wow, I won't last through much of this. Every moan and grunt stokes the heat and pressure building between my legs. He's clearly enjoying himself, which turns me on so much it makes me dizzy.

"Daddy, please," I beg, my legs trembling. He cranes his head up to answer me, circling my clit with his thumb as he fingers me.

"Not yet, baby girl," he growls. A second finger stretches me open, hitting my pleasure center with each curling stroke.

I'm using every ounce of strength to hold my orgasm back. My muscles are tense from head to toe, my body dewy with sweat as I clench down on his strong fingers.

"Daddy, please!" I wail desperately.

"Five," he growls before drawing my clit in between his lips.

Oh fuck. We've played like this over video chat. When I masturbate, I imagine his lips against my ear, counting me down to climax.

This is much, much harder.

"Four." He laps at my clit in time with his fingers, picking up the pace with both.

I'm pressurized as a shaken soda. All I need is Daddy's permission to take that cap off and let my erupt.

"Three." I grip the sheets tight in my fists.

"Two," he growls.

"One. Come for me, baby girl. Come for Daddy," he commands before he sucks my clit between his lips and licks vigorously. I break open and he rips every ounce of pleasure from my body.

My climax crashes over me like a deluge through a broken dam. All of the tension I held while I was edging melts away under each warm, tingling wave. It feels like my body is weightless and spacious as the pleasure ebbs into a diffused afterglow.

Wayne rears up with a devilish, satisfied grin on his face. He wipes his chin lewdly then curls up beside me, pulling me close.

He kisses me deeply and I taste my own satisfaction on his tongue. His face smells like my sweet musk.

"I love you, Daddy," I murmur as he lays my head against his chest.

Oh, shit. "...Um, not because of what just happened!" I add stupidly.

That busts him up. His hearty laugh echoes through me. He has to wipe a tear from his eye before he composes himself.

"I'm sorry, sweetheart," he chuckles. "That was a good one."

He tilts my face up so that our eyes lock.

"I love you too, Elyse." His earnest eyes shine with emotion.

I sniffle as a happy tear trails down my cheek. He's more than I'd ever hoped for. We cling tight to one another and fall asleep embraced.

EPILOGUE

Elyse

I was walking around like a cowgirl after Wayne's last day in town. He took me in the kitchen, on the couch, in the shower. It didn't take long for us to christen my whole apartment.

I started looking for jobs in Chicago the night he left. I wanted to wait until the next day but I couldn't resist. I'd never been more sure of anything as I am about my future with Wayne.

A small gallery hired me and I've fallen in love with the city. The old architecture always catches my eye. More than once I've bumped into someone because I was staring up at the buildings like a yokel.

It's been about a year and a half now. The splendor hasn't worn off, but I've adapted to the pace of city life. Wayne's helped me learn to cook and I'm feeling better than ever. I still can't eat out much, but that stings less as my cooking gets better!

My life is going better than I'd ever imagined. Today, though, I think I'm in for it.

Wayne and I have a chore chart at home for me. I like to spoil him, so it's things I'd likely take care of anyway. So why not get credit for it and maybe a reward here and there?

Except yesterday I decided to blow it off. I ignored every single duty and spent the day making crafts and playing in little space.

Daddy wasn't happy to come home to such a big mess. Once he made sure that I wasn't upset, he had me write lines and promised me a spanking today.

His keys rattle in the door and a chill runs over my skin. Goosebumps spring up as he enters, looking like a centerfold come to life in his fitted charcoal suit.

"There's my naughty girl," he purrs, slipping off his tie. "Get into position in the bedroom, love. I'll be in in a minute."

"Yes, Daddy," I answer. I practically skip back to the bedroom.

Maybe I wanted to get this spanking on purpose. My body vibrates with excitement as I lean over the bed, my ass poking out over the edge.

When Daddy enters he's dressed in his slacks and a black tank top. I actually drool a little at the sight of him but I catch it just in time. He's so fucking hot.

He stands behind me and runs his hand over my panties.

"Already wet," he rasps, teasing my slit lazily over the fabric.

"Yes, Daddy," I whine. His gentle touch is already unraveling me.

"Why are you being punished, my love?" he coos as he grips my behind roughly, kneading one cheek and then the other.

"For ignoring my chores, Daddy." He squeezes so hard that I whimper with delight.

I love feeling his power, being at his mercy. I can release completely because I know I'm safe and loved.

"That's right," he says as the first swat lands.

Sharp pain cuts through me as his blows fall hard on one cheek, then the other. The sting turns into a burn, then into a pulsing, scorching ache.

"How's my girl doing?" He asks as he pauses the onslaught to rub my pussy.

"Good, Daddy," I pant. I'm swimming in endorphins and loving every second of it.

"Good girl. Ten more," he states.

Ten?! Before I can react, the swats fall hard and fast on my behind. There's no tears today — I didn't do anything too bad. So I just ride the euphoria and enjoy every drop of the intense sensations.

"All done, sweetheart," he coos, rubbing my lower back. I'm panting into the bed, smiling wide as he runs his palms over my searing, aching behind.

"So fucking sexy like this, Elyse. Soaking wet and beet red." I cry out when he teases up and down my slit, slicking his finger with my excitement and sliding it sensuously over my clit.

"Do you want more, baby girl?" he rasps, unbuckling his slacks. I hear the quiet hiss of fabric slipping down his legs and my body lights up.

"Yes, Daddy, please!" I beg, wiggling my hips back and forth slightly.

He slides in to the hilt, stretching me open suddenly. My body is ready for him and pulls him in greedily, making us both moan in delight.

"That's my good girl," he purrs. "Take Daddy's cock."

I howl and moan in response to his deep pumps. His hips slam into mine with a loud slapping sound that rings through the room.

"So wet. So tight. Fucking perfect, baby girl," he growls as he lowers down over me, his breath hot on my cheek.

Each move hits my pleasure center as he thrusts hard, burying himself inside me with each pump.

Pleasure pours over me, making me feel tingly and floaty.

"Play with yourself," he commands. That stern tone rings through me like a bell. I obey, slipping my hand beneath me to circle my clit.

I wail as he fucks me mercilessly, just how I like. I'm helpless under him and it feels heavenly. Heat and pressure in my belly let me know my climax is near.

"Let it go, baby girl," he grunts. "Come for me. Come all over Daddy's cock."

My body responds immediately, setting my orgasm free. I tremble and quake as sparks erupt from every cell.

"So fucking hot for Daddy," he growls. Those dark, wild eyes take in my every movement.

"You're gonna make me come, Elyse," he strains, his cock twitching inside me.

"Show me, Daddy, please," I beg. I'm equally shocked and pleased by my own filthy mouth.

He pulls out and roars as he comes, stroking himself as he shoots hot ropes of satisfaction all over my chest and belly. It's an intoxicating sight.

"All mine," he pants, looking me over. He trails a finger down my body, through his tribute, reveling in the filthy mess we've made.

Wayne plucks his boxers off of the floor and wipes my midsection down.

"We have towels, you know," I tease, pointing to the closet.

He gives me a playful side eye and grabs one, then heads into the bathroom.

A moment later he returns with a warm, wet cloth and cleans me up. "My beautiful girl," he murmurs as he wipes between my legs.

He gets into bed and curls me up into him so that we're spooning. He twiddles my hair as he showers me with praise. His precious girl, the champ of taking a spanking.

"I have a feeling you acted up on purpose," he drawls in my ear, running his hand over my sore bottom.

"Yeah, maybe," I tease, wriggling against him.

"You're always my good girl, you know that?" he asks as his finger traces down the contour of my side.

"I know, Daddy," I reply. "I love you."

"I love you too, sweet girl."

Riding With Daddy

Neither Rory nor June expected to find true love along the side of a rural highway. But when he came across June, soaked to the bone and all alone in the world, he couldn't ignore his Daddy Dom instinct. She needed his protection.

On their journey, lust blooms into love. June experiences deep submission for the first time as Rory's little girl. Look inside for your next short, steamy, DDlg instalove BDSM romance!

Daddy's Security

If you give a brat a curfew, you're going to have to give her some discipline to go with it.

Elle, a spoiled, melancholy starlet, can't believe that gruff Leroy won't bend to her will. Her huge, surly security guard is the first person in her life to give her any boundaries. Or tries to, at least.

When Elle puts herself in danger, Leroy has to grapple with his dominant, Daddy side being pulled to this reckless little girl. Can they deny the magnetism between them? Emotional, raw, and plenty spicy, this quick instalove romance is lavish as the Hollywood Hills.

Reunited With Daddy

Persephone lost her Daddy a long time ago. He was pulled away for work and she needed to stay to take care of her ailing aunt. Forlorn, she aches for her lost love when she attends a friend's wedding. A friend who found her forever Daddy Dom.

When Persephone leaves the ceremony, she runs into the person she least expected. Her Daddy, William, is handsome as ever, even ten years later. The two rekindle their long lost love and celebrate with hot, naughty play time. Enjoy a heartfelt, romantic journey that ends in Daddy's arms in this short, steamy, discipline erotica.

Fated: A Ddlg, Abdl, Instalove Erotic Romance

Wendy is at the end of her rope. She's lost everything because of who she is: a little. No job, no family, nothing to keep her off of the roof of her twenty story apartment building. Except Shawn.

The gruff, rugged veteran has faced indescribable darkness himself. He sees Wendy's pain. He won't let her face her problems without backup. She can't help but fall for the way this huge, dominant man dotes on her tenderly. Heartfelt, raw, and steamy —this hot BDSM romance between an ABDL baby girl and her loving Daddy Dom will have you begging for more!

Content note: This story contains discussion of suicidality and suicidal ideation.

Ranger Daddy

Environmental activism. A shrewd oil company. A surly forest ranger and a lookout tower.

These are the ingredients in the sh*t smoothie Ashley walks into at an anti-drilling protest. Feisty and idealistic, Ashley bites back against the gruff, dominant forest ranger. When violence erupts, she finds herself helpless in his strong arms. Alone in the ranger tower, Ashley and ranger Christopher struggle for power. How did he end up taking care of this wild little brat? And will she get her way and finally find the Daddy Dom she's been searching for? See how their steamy story unfolds in this quick instalove, daddy dom discipline erotica.

THANK YOU FOR READING

Thank you so much for supporting my work. I love writing about this lifestyle and you make it possible!

Want a FREE eBook? Sign up for my newsletter to receive an exclusive story!! Plus sneak-peaks and snippets of my upcoming work! No spam, ever — pinkie swear.

Follow me on Amazon Author Central to stay up to date on my publications!

'Til next time,
Sonia